Little Einsteins, Music of the Meadow photo credits: Fluffy clouds © Craig Aurness/Corbis; Grassy hill and fields © W. Cody/Corbis; Rustic stairwell © Melanie Acevedo/Botanica; Scenic view of a waterfall on Havasu Creek © Wilbur E. Garrett/National Geographic; Farm, Peacham, Vermont, USA © Panoramic Images; Meadow of wildflowers © William A. Bake/ Corbis; Fireweed Mendenhall Glacier, Juneau, Alaska, USA © Panoramic Images; Alpine landscape of lupine-covered meadow, Olympic National Park, Washington © Darrell Gulin/ Botanica; Fountain of Four Evangelists in central courtyard of San Juan Capistrano © Stephen Saks/Lonely Planet Images; Golf course, Manalee Bay, Lanai Hawaii, USA © Panoramic Images; Landscape reflecting in lake, Norway © Howard Kingsnorth/zefa/Corbis; Regal lilies in garden © Mark Bolton/Corbis; Man standing at waterfall, Bavaria, Germany © Uli Wiesmeier/zefa/Corbis; Moeraki Boulders, stones on beach near Oamaru, New Zealand © Wilfried Krecichwost/zefa/Corbis; Tree frog sitting on a branch © Theo Allofs/zefa/Corbis; Vintgar Gorge, Slovenia © Roland Gerth/zefa/Corbis; Cascading by the wildflowers © Craig Tuttle/Corbis; Glacial erratics on prairie © Tom Bean/Corbis; Doorway of patriotic home © Strauss/Curtis/Corbis; Young man jumping out of water © Parque/zefa/Corbis; Shallow water at shore of lake © Ron Watts/Corbis; Upper Multnomah Falls © Craig Tuttle/Corbis; Tree-frog tadpole © Michael & Patricia Fogden/Corbis; Red-eyed leaf-frog tadpoles © Michael & Patricia Fogden/Corbis; Western green tree frog leaping from tree trunk © David A. Northcott/Corbis; Serious bullfrog © Randy M. Ury/Corbis; Snorkeling off Bora-Bora © Patrick Ward/Corbis; A chipmunk eats a nut © Taylor S. Kennedy/National Geographic; Black panther on a tree branch © John Conrad/Corbis; Eastern American chipmunk © Gary W. Carter/Corbis; Brugmansia hangs over mixed floral bed © Marion Brenner/Botanica; A captive birdwing butterfly lands on a pink flower © Roy Toft/National Geographic; Close view of a blue and yellow glassy tiger butterfly on a pink flower © Timothy Laman/National Geographic; Panoramic view of field of poppies and wild flowers near Montchiello, Tuscany, Italy, Europe © Lee Frost/Robert Harding World Imagery; Chestnut trees in the autumn © Herbert Kehrer/ zefa/Corbis; Butterflies flying © Thom Lang/Corbis; Three baby robins in a nest Wilmington, Delaware © Lisa J. Goodman/The Image Bank; Robin (Erithacus rubecula) © Pal Hermansen/ The Image Bank; Close-up of the feather-shaped leaves of many glossy leaflets of the evergreen, slender palm Chamaedorea elegans, Neanthe Bella Dwarf mountain palm, Parlour palm © Dorling Kindersley/Dorling Kindersley; A chipmunk eats a nut © Taylor S. Kennedy/National Geographic; Man standing at waterfall, Bavaria, Germany © Uli Wiesmeier/zefa/Corbis; Red-bellied woodpecker sitting at a hole on the tree trunk © Markus Botzek/zefa/Corbis; Coral Pink Sand Dunes State Park, Utah © Massimo Mastrorillo/Corbis; Grasshopper © H. Zettl/zefa/Corbis; Eggs in bird's nest © Burke/Triolo Productions/Brand X Pictures; Bee zooming to Iceland poppy © Taesam Do/Botanica; Buffy fish-owl, Ketupa-ketupa, perched on a branch facing the viewer © Cyril Laubscher/Dorling Kindersley; Wildflowers © Annie Griffiths Belt/National Geographic; Close view of a blue and yellow glassy tiger butterfly on a pink flower © Timothy Laman/National Geographic; Grand Teton Park, Wyoming, USA © Panoramic Images; Teenage boy fishing at lake © Caterina Bernardi/zefa/Corbis; Butterfly Collection © G. Schuster/zefa/Corbis; Robin on branch © Christof Wermter/zefa/Corbis; Bat flying at night © F. Rauschenbach/zefa/Corbis; Owl © H. Spichtinger/zefa/Corbis; Eastern American chipmunk examining a wild mushroom © Orion Press/Corbis; Little brown bat in flight © Joe McDonald/Corbis; Leaf-nosed bat flying in night © Joe McDonald/Corbis; Atlas moth above other moths and butterflies © Darrell Gulin/Corbis; Meadow of wildflowers © William A. Bake/Corbis; Rolling green hills against sky © Terry W. Eggers/Corbis; Maize field and flowers © Gallo Images; Orange poppy sways © Botanica; Meadow of spring wildflowers, including California poppies (Eschscholzia californica) and owl's clover (Orthocarpus), Antelope Valley, California, USA © Visuals Unlimited; Baby bird in nest © The Image Bank; Fern Leaves © Iconica; Broken robin's egg in empty bird's nest © Taxi; Leaves on branch © Photonica

First published by Parragon in 2009

Parragon
Queen Street House
4 Queen Street
Bath BA1 1HE, UK

Copyright © 2009 Disney Enterprises, Inc.

ISBN 978-1-4075-6034-2

Printed in China

PLAYHOUSE
STORYBOOK
COLLECTION

PaRragon

Bath · New York · Singapore · Hong Kong · Cologne · Delhi · Melbourne

TABLE OF CONTENTS

MICKEY

GOOFY

STARRING

DONALD

DAISY

PLUTO

MINNIE

UP, UP AND AWAY!

Donald and his friends were standing outside the
Clubhouse on a crisp, bright day.

"Oh, Donald," Daisy said, "look at the sky! It's lovely!"

"Shhh!" Donald whispered. "Don't make a move! Something
is following me and I'm going to find out who, or what, it is!"

Daisy giggled as she looked behind Donald. "Oh, my!" said Daisy. "There is something following you! It's wearing a sailor's cap – just like yours. It's got cute webbed feet – just like yours. And when you move, it moves, too."

"Aw, phooey," Donald quacked as he turned around and saw his shadow. "That is a fine-looking shape, but I still don't trust it!"

The friends laughed at Donald as he glared at his shadow.

"Cheer up, buddy," Mickey said. "Why don't you leave your shadow on the ground and come with me?"

"I don't know." Donald moped. "Where are we going?"

"Up, up and away!" Mickey cheered. "Who wants to help Minnie and me fly our hot-air balloon?"

"I sure do!" shouted Goofy.

"You can count me out," Donald grumbled. "I don't trust that thing. Besides," he added, "I'm not missing lunch."

"Aw, come on, Donald," Minnie pleaded, "I've packed a square meal for each of us. Up, up and away!"

13

"Something's wrong," Mickey said. "The balloon won't fill with air!"

"That's too bad, buddy," said Donald, trying to hide a grin.

"I guess we'll just have to go back to the Clubhouse for lunch."

"Oh, Toodles!" Mickey said. "Do we have a Mousetool that can help?"

Toodles appeared. "Do any of you know how we can use this tool?" Mickey asked.

"I know, Mickey!" answered Minnie. "We can turn the crank to inflate the balloon with hot air."

"Why, you're right, Minnie!"
Mickey shouted.
"We've got ears!
Say cheers!"

15

Soon, the friends were floating high above the Clubhouse.
"Up, up and away!" cried Daisy. "This is fun!"
"Look, everyone!" yelled Minnie. "Can you see the Clubhouse
from here? It looks so small! And there are so many shapes below
us. I see a heart, a triangle and a rectangle. What do you see?"

"I see a triangle, too!" Mickey shouted. "And there are Chip and Dale playing a round of golf!"

"It should be called a triangle of golf," laughed Daisy. "Just look at all those triangle-shaped flags!"

"What's a triangle?" asked Goofy, as he bit into his sandwich.

"A triangle is a shape with three sides that all have points at the ends – sort of like your sandwich," Minnie explained.

"Or like that?" Goofy questioned, as he pointed to a huge triangle in front of the balloon.

It was the top of a mountain! Suddenly, a gust of wind whisked the friends right towards it!

"We need help," cried Mickey. "Oh, Toodles!"

Toodles appeared with a triangle, a patch, a ladder and a telescope.

"Which tool should we use?" asked Minnie.

"All of them!" said Mickey. "Daisy, ring the triangle for help!"

Daisy rang the triangle, but it didn't help them get off the mountain.

"Minnie, patch the hole!"

Minnie put a square patch on the round hole in the balloon, but it was too small.

"Goofy, look through the telescope!" Goofy held the telescope and saw that the ground looked very far away.

"There's only one tool left," yelled Mickey. "To the ladder!"

Mickey dropped the ladder over the side of the balloon.

"We've got ears! Say cheers!" said Mickey. "If we can't get the balloon to go back up, then we'll have to go down – one step at a time."

"Me first! Me first!" shouted Donald.

"We're going to do this fair and square," Mickey announced.

"Take a piece of paper with a number on it. Whoever gets number 1 goes first. Whoever gets number 2 goes second. Get the idea?"

The friends headed down the ladder one by one. Everyone was happy to be standing on firm ground again. "We're in great shape, unlike our balloon," said Mickey. "But we're going to have to hike back home. It's not far – just down that path . . .
                    or maybe it's that one."

The friends trudged along, growing more and more tired.

"I think we've been walking in circles," Mickey finally said.

"I'm sure I've seen this tree before."

"Oh, Toodles!" Toodles appeared, showing three pictures of Mickey. Mickey shared them with his friends.

"I'm standing in front of the Clubhouse and my shadow is different in each picture. In the morning, my shadow falls in front of me. At noon, I have no shadow. In the evening, my shadow falls behind me. Do any of you know what this could mean?"

28

The friends studied the pictures carefully.

"I've got it!" Donald shouted. "Right now, it's late and the sun is setting behind us. Toodles shows that in the evening, our shadows point towards the Clubhouse. If we follow them, they'll lead us back home."

Donald was correct. The shadows helped the friends head in the right direction. Soon, they arrived back at the Clubhouse. Everyone was hungry from the long trip.

"Well, Donald," Daisy said, "do you trust your shadow now?"

"I'll trust the handsome guy to lead me home," Donald answered. "But he'd better not ask me to share my pie!"

MANNY

DUSTY

STRETCH

SQUEEZE

STARRING

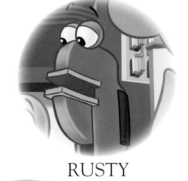

RUSTY

PAT

FELIPE

TURNER

The Best Repairman

His repair shop had only been open for a few minutes, but Manny already had his first customer of the day. It was Gabriela.

On her walk through the park that morning, she noticed that Sparrow Fountain was broken.

"I found the statue's beak on the ground," Gabriela explained. "It must have broken off during the big storm last night."

"Thanks, Gabriela," said Manny. "The tools and I will have it fixed in no time."

As soon as Gabriela left the shop, Manny ran to answer the phone. "Handy Manny's Repair Shop. You break it, we fix it!"

"Manny? It's Jasmine Chung from the Sheet Rock Hills Herald. I'm calling to tell you that you've been picked as the county's best repairman!"

Manny couldn't believe it. "Wow, me? Gracias, that's very nice of you!"

Jasmine explained that she was writing a story about Manny and wanted to interview him at his next repair job.

"A reporter is coming to interview me at the park!" Manny told the tools once he'd hung up with Jasmine.

"Cool! A reporter!" Pat shouted. "Uh, what's a reporter?"

"A reporter is someone who writes stories in the periódico, the newspaper," explained Felipe. "And she's going to write a story about us!"

"That's right, Felipe, but first we need to buy some supplies so we can repair Sparrow Fountain," said Manny.

Where does Manny usually buy his supplies? Yes, at Kelly's Hardware Store!

On his way to the hardware store, Manny passed Mr Lopart, who was squirting something onto his door. "Hola, Mister Lopart! Is there something wrong with your door?"

"Well, on hot days like today, it just swells up and doesn't close right." Mr Lopart grunted, pushing the door with all his might. "But I put a little grease on it, so it should be as good as neeeewwwww – oof!"

Mr Lopart slipped on the grease and fell onto the pavement! Manny helped him get back up.

"We could help fix your door after our newspaper interview," Manny offered.

"No, Manny, I don't need any – NEWSPAPER INTERVIEW?!" Mr Lopart shouted.

Stretch beamed with pride. "Yes. The Sheet Rock Hills Herald named Manny the best repairman in the whole county!"

"We're meeting the reporter in the park, but first we need to get to the hardware store. Adiós!" said Manny.

Hmm, thought Mr Lopart, if I bring some of my candy to the park and let the reporter try it, maybe she'll name me the county's best sweet maker right on the spot!

At the hardware store, Manny talked to Kelly about his big interview, while the tools looked for supplies.

"Let's see," Dusty said, looking around the shop. "We need to find just the right item for the job."

"You said it, Dusty!" Pat agreed. "Um, what job is that?"

Turner scowled, "Sparrow Fountain, you hammerhead! We need to stick the beak back on the statue of the bird, remember?"

Stretch scanned the shelves. "Hmmm, what should we use to secure the beak to the statue? Should we go with Easy-Tie String, Strong 'n' Sticky Grout or the Shiny Bright Paint?"

Which item is the best one for the job?

"Well, most statues are heavy because they're made of stone," Felipe pointed out. "So I don't think string is strong enough to hold the heavy beak in place."

"And paint won't help – it will just make the beak colourful," said Rusty.

"So, it must be the Strong 'n' Sticky Grout that we need!" shouted Squeeze. "Hooray! We figured it out!"

Manny grinned. "Great job, tools!"

After ringing up Manny's purchase at the cash register, Kelly showed everyone her framed newspaper article. "You know, the newspaper did an article on me when I first opened the hardware store."

"Wow, they put your picture in the paper and everything!" marvelled Pat.

"Will we get our picture in the paper, too, Manny?" shrieked Dusty.

"Maybe," answered Manny.

The tools couldn't contain their excitement and started hopping all around the hardware store.

Once they got to the park, Manny inspected the damage to Sparrow Fountain.

"Hmm, looks like the pipes inside the fountain are broken, too," noted Manny. "All the water has drained out."

This made Squeeze sad. "Aww, the birds that come here have nothing to drink."

"You're right, Squeeze, but we can fix it!" promised Manny.

"Of course we can, Manny. And the reporter can take a photo of us repairing the fountain!" said Felipe. "Ooh, I hope I look extra shiny for my big newspaper picture!"

Just then, a woman raced over to the fountain. "Manny! Jasmine Chung here," she said quickly. "Ready for the interview? Yes? Yes! Okay, then. Take a seat! Let's get to it!"

"Yikes, she talks so fast that I'm starting to get dizzy," Rusty whispered to Pat.

"Well, I should really take care of the repairs first . . ." Manny started to say.

"Oh, this will only take a few minutes!" Jasmine interrupted, fiddling with her tape recorder. "We'll just zip through it, I promise, and then you can get right to work! Super idea, right? Yes! Let's get started, shall we?"

"Um, okay . . ." said Manny, a little unsure.

"Great!" Jasmine exclaimed, pressing the record button on her tape recorder. "So, did you always want to be a repairman?"

"Oh, yes." Manny grinned. "My parents tell me that 'fix' was my very first word!"

"That's a great quote," Jasmine said. "I may even put that under your picture!"

"Picture?!" shouted Dusty, as she and the other tools started to gather around Manny.

Squeeze shrieked, "If we say something great, will you put our pictures in the paper, too?!"

"I just might!" answered Jasmine.

"Then my picture's going in the paper for sure," boasted Turner, "because everything I say is great!"

"Don't listen to him – he's got a screw loose," Felipe sneered. "I, however, can twist and turn like no other. Plus, I'm really, really shiny!"

In their struggle to get Jasmine's attention, Turner and Felipe crashed into Jasmine's tape recorder. It fell to the ground, causing a button to fly off.

Manny picked up the tape recorder and quickly snapped the button back into place.

Jasmine was amazed. "Thanks, Manny. Nice work!"

"As for you two," Manny said to Turner and Felipe. "You have to be more careful."

"Sí," whispered Felipe, feeling embarrassed.

"Okay," Turner sighed.

"Maybe everyone will be a little more relaxed after we fix the fuente," suggested Manny.

"A fuente?! We can't fix a fuente now, Manny!" stammered Pat.

"We have to fix the fountain!"

"Fuente is Spanish for 'fountain', Pat."

Stretch giggled.

"First we have to repair the waterspout inside the fountain," observed Manny. "So, I'll need Rusty to help me with that."

Jasmine got her camera ready. "Great! An action shot like that is sure to make it into the paper!"

"Photo in the paper?" said Felipe, jumping in front of the camera. "What good is a photo without something shiny in it?"

Not wanting to miss out on the photo, Turner pushed Felipe aside and was soon joined by Dusty, who was practising all her best poses.

Soon all the tools were hopping around Jasmine, showing off their special talents. Stretch jumped on top of her head to take measurements, while Pat hammered the ground around Jasmine's feet. Squeeze tried to crush an acorn, but instead sent it flying into Jasmine's leg!

"Yikes!" screeched Jasmine.

51

"Tools – STOP!" Manny ordered. "I know you want your pictures in the paper, but you're forgetting why Jasmine wants our picture in the periódico to begin with."

"Because I'm so shiny, sí?" asked Felipe.

"No, Felipe," Manny continued, "because we help others by fixing things. But we can't help anyone if you're all too busy smiling and posing."

The tools felt bad about the way they had acted.

"This fountain is broken, and the birds can't get a drink on a hot day like today," said Manny. "So, instead of worrying about getting our picture in the paper, let's think about why we're really here."

"To help others!" cheered Dusty. "Let's get going and fix it right!"

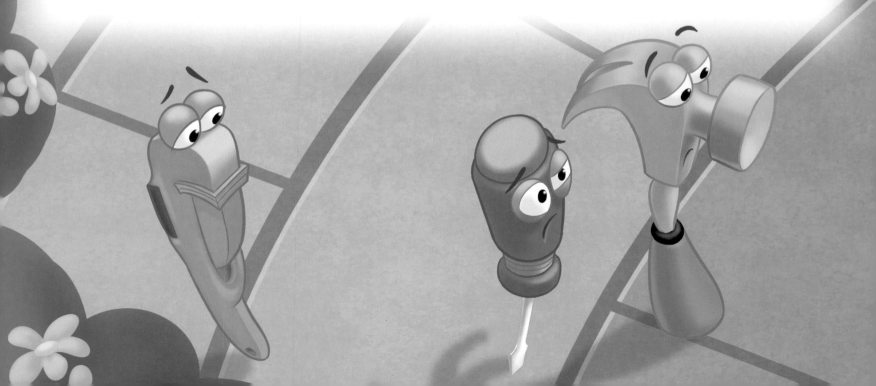

Manny and the tools worked together to fix the fountain.

"Wow, Manny, you really are the county's best repairman!" raved Jasmine. "Sparrow Fountain looks as good as new!"

"Look, the birds are returning to the fountain!" Rusty said.

Manny smiled. "Magnífico! More happy customers!"

"Okay, now that the fountain is fixed, let's get back to our interview," suggested Jasmine. "I don't think we need to worry about any more interruptions –"

"Wait! Stop!" shouted Mr Lopart, frantically pushing a wheelbarrow filled with sweets towards Jasmine. "Interview me, too! I'm the county's best sweets maker – WHOOPS!"

Mr Lopart's wheelbarrow hit a rock, and a big puff of sticky candyfloss landed right on Jasmine's head!

Manny chuckled. "Jasmine, you may want to track down the county's best hairdresser for your next interview!"

The following week, Manny flipped through the newspaper to find Jasmine's article.

"There it is! There's the picture!" yelled Squeeze.

Turner was surprised. "Hey, we're all in it!"

"Sí, I may be the county's best repairman, but you're the county's best tools!" Manny said. "We make a great team!"

POOH

PIGLET

RABBIT

TIGGER

BUSTER

DARBY

The Colour Case

One day in the Hundred-Acre Wood, Pooh, Piglet and Rabbit were painting the backdrop for their new play: *The Busy Buzzy Bees.*

"A bright blue sky," said Rabbit.

"A pretty red flower," said Piglet.

"A friendly yellow bee," said Pooh, "who will visit the red flower, then fly through the blue sky to the big honey tree."

"Hmmmm…" pondered Pooh. "Honey trees make me think of honey. And that makes my tummy rumbly. Piglet and Rabbit, do you suppose it might be that time of day when a snack would be nice?"

"Indeed!" agreed Rabbit.

"Yes, yes, yes!" said Piglet.

"That is just what I was supposing," said Pooh.

So the three painters left the scene to enjoy an afternoon snack.

Upon their return, Pooh, Piglet and Rabbit saw a strange sight.

"My, my," said Piglet. "Where did these colours come from?"

"It would appear," said Rabbit, "that *someone* has trespassed on our stage! Someone with purple paint, orange paint… and green paint!"

"But who?" puzzled Piglet. "This is certainly a mystery."

"And mysteries call for Super Sleuths!" announced Pooh.
"I'll go sound the alarm!"

Pooh sounded the Super Siren…

SSSuuuUUPPPPPerrrSSlilEEUUtthhs!

… and raised the Finder Flag!

69

The Super Sleuths – Darby, Tigger, Pooh and Buster, too – all met in front of the Changing Tree.

"It looks like there's a mystery at the new theatre," said Darby.

"That so?" asked Tigger. "I thought *The Busy Buzzy Bees* was a comedy."

"I mean," said Darby, "that the Finder Flag has a picture of the stage on it."

"Yes," piped up Pooh. "The theatre has a rather mysterious guest – a colourful one, I might add."

"Come on, then," proclaimed Darby. "Let's solve this mystery!"

"Any time, any place,
The Super Sleuths are on the case!"

"We left for a snack…" started Piglet.

"And when we came back…" added Pooh.

"We saw all these tracks!" said Rabbit. "We only had yellow, blue and red paint."

"And now there are green, purple and orange tracks on the stage," said Darby.

"This gives me stage fright!" said Piglet, shivering.

"Think, think, think!" said Darby. "Who else would have paint in the Hundred-Acre Wood? And how did the colours get onto the stage?"

"Yap, yap, yap!" barked Buster.

"What is it, Buster?" said Darby. "Are you paw-painting?"

"Hoo-hoo!" cried Tigger. "New paint tracks!"

"But those are Buster's tracks," said Piglet. "So… Buster must be the mystery painter."

"Let me look into this more closely…" said Tigger. "Aha!
It appears that Buster has two-stepped into blue and waltzed
into yellow – and made some very nice green puppy pawprints! You've got
talent, Buster boy!"

"That's it!" said Darby! "When you mix blue and yellow,
it makes green!"

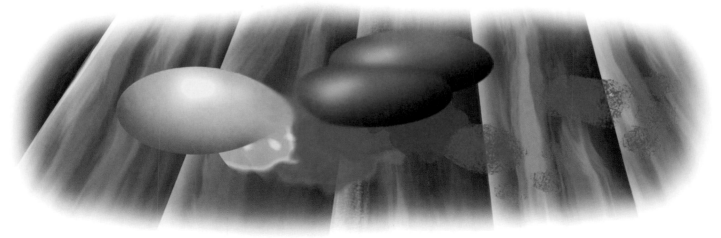

"I do believe," said Pooh, "that Buster is not the only one with green feet. Oh, bother."

"Silly ol' bear," said Darby. "You must have walked in blue and yellow paint – and made these big green tracks."

"Oh, my, oh, my, oh, my…" sighed Rabbit.

"Mine, too," nodded Piglet.

Darby smiled. "So, *you* two have stepped in paint! Let's see…
what two colours make purple? And what makes orange? Let's find out!"

"Look!" said Piglet. "When red and yellow mix, they make orange. I must have stepped in both colours and made those orange tracks."

"A tiggerific colour, I might add," added Tigger.

"Well, well," said Rabbit, "I must have stepped in red and blue – because they make purple."

"Mystery solved!" announced Tigger.

"And look at this," said Darby. "When all three mix together, they make brown! Hmmm... this gives me an idea..."

All the friends worked together. With only three cans of paint,
they made enough colours to create the perfect backdrop for...

...one funny, honeyful comedy.
And another mystery was history.

LOOK BEFORE YOU LEAP!

Mickey and Goofy were enjoying a quiet game of chess. Just as Mickey was about to make a move, something soared through the window and landed right in the middle of the chessboard.

"What was that?" Mickey asked.

The two friends looked carefully at something that looked right back at them. It was green. It had webbed feet. It said, "Ribbit, ribbit."

It was a frog – a very jumpy frog. Goofy tried to grab it. *PLOP!*
The frog leaped out of Goofy's hands and right onto the silly switch.
The room began to spin around. Mickey tried to grab the frog,
but it leaped right towards the . . .

. . . kitchen sink. *KERPLUNK!*

"You really should look before you leap!" Mickey said to the frog.

"What are we going to do about this big puddle?" Goofy asked.

"Oh, Toodles!" Mickey called. "We need some Mouseketools –
right now!"

"The mop is the right tool for this job," said Mickey. "Thanks, Toodles!" All of Mickey's hard work made Goofy hungry. He decided to make lunch. Just then, the frog took a giant leap right towards . . .

. . . Goofy's sandwich. *SQUISH!*

"Stop!" Mickey cried as Goofy was about to take a bite.

"You really should look before you leap," Goofy said to the frog. "And I should look before I bite!"

89

Goofy carried the frog outside.

"Hold on tight," Mickey said. "He's pretty slippery."

"I have him. . . I have him. . . *OOPS!* I don't have him!"

Goofy yelped as the frog leaped right towards . . .

. . . Daisy's painting! *SPLAT!*

"You should look before you leap!" Daisy said as the paint splattered everywhere. "Now my painting – and my clothes – are a mess."

91

"Hey there, little friend," Mickey said to the frog. "Slow down!"

But it was too late. The frog leaped out from behind Daisy's painting and headed straight towards . . .

. . . Mickey's bicycle. *BOING!* He zoomed down the road, holding tightly to the handlebars. He was heading straight for a cliff.

"Oh, no!" Goofy shouted.

"Oh, Toodles!" yelled Mickey. "We need you!"

"The lasso is the right tool for this job," said Mickey. "Thanks, Toodles!"

Mickey and Goofy carefully pulled the bicycle back from the edge of the cliff.

"I think we should help our friend the frog find a nice, safe pond," Mickey said. "Then he can leap without causing any trouble."

The frog jumped up and down in agreement. Then he hopped away down the road with Mickey and Goofy following behind him.

The frog stopped hopping right in front of the pizzeria.

Slowly, Mickey and Goofy crept up behind him.

"We've got to get him before he leaps!" Mickey whispered.

But it was too late. Just as Mickey reached for him, the frog leaped right onto a . . .

. . . pizza. *SLOSH!*

"You should look before you leap!" shouted the man behind the counter, as tomato sauce dripped off the pizza. The frog stopped for a moment to lick himself off. Then he hopped down Main Street, heading right towards Minnie and Pluto.

"Maybe Minnie and Pluto can help us catch our frog friend and take him to a nice pond," Mickey shouted.

But the frog had other ideas. He took a great big leap and landed right inside . . .

. . . the goldfish bowl. *SPLASH!* The big wave made the
goldfish fly right out. Minnie gently put the goldfish back into its bowl.

"I don't know if we'll ever find a pond for froggie. We need some help!"
Goofy sighed.

"Oh, Toodles!" Mickey called.

"The net is the right tool for this job," said Mickey. At last, they held the frog safely in the net.

"He seems sad," Goofy said.

"I think you're right, Goofy," Mickey agreed. Then he looked up ahead and saw something that made him, and the frog, smile.

"I think we've found just the right place for you, froggie," Mickey said.

The friends walked quickly down the street towards the fountain.
Carefully, Mickey placed the net on the ground and began to lift the frog
out. But the frog was impatient.

Out he hopped, heading straight for the . . .

. . . fountain. He landed with a *SWOOSH!* right next to another frog.

"Ribbit, ribbit," he said.

"Ribbit, ribbit," she replied.

"Maybe we didn't find a pond," said Mickey, "but we did find a good place for him to splash and leap."

"We've found the frog a friend, too," noticed Minnie. "And they look very happy to see each other!"

"I think Minnie's goldfish is happy, too!" added Goofy.

Later, while Donald, Minnie and Daisy made dinner,
Mickey and Goofy got back to their game of chess.

"C'mon, Mickey," Goofy said, "you haven't made a move in a long time."

"I know, I know," replied Mickey. "I just want to make sure I look carefully before I leap!"

Elliot Minds the Store

Manny and the tools had a busy week ahead of them.

"Putting the work schedule up here will definitely help the shop run more smoothly," Manny said as he tacked the schedule to the bulletin board. "Thanks for the great idea, Stretch."

Stretch blushed. "Aw, well, it's really no big deal."

"You can say that again," grumbled Turner. "Hmmph! Anyone could have come up with that idea!"

"You didn't!" Felipe reminded Turner.

"Yeah, well…that's because I was too busy coming up with an even better way to organize the workshop!" Turner said with a sneer.

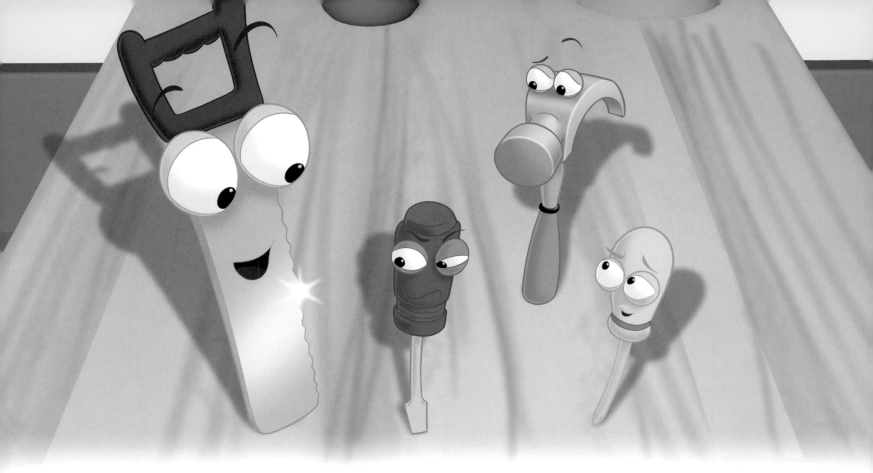

Felipe rolled his eyes. "Well, come on, Turner. The world is waiting to hear this most intelligent idea from the sharpest tool in the toolbox!"

"That's funny." Pat smiled. "People are always telling me that I'm not the sharpest tool in the toolbox, which makes sense since I don't have any sharp points!"

"You can say that again," Felipe muttered.

"Gee, I think I win for sharpest points," Dusty said with a laugh. "But, okay, go ahead with your big idea, Turner."

Turner started to cough and clear his throat. "Ahem, let's see…okay…er…ooh, I know! Let's take all the paperwork, put it on a clipboard and then hang the clipboard on the bulletin board!"

Felipe yawned. "Ho-hum, speaking of 'bored'…"

"Well, it can't hurt to try!" suggested Manny. He tacked the clipboard to the bulletin board.

But within a few seconds, the whole bulletin board came crashing to the floor!

Stretch peered out from under a sheet of paper. "I hope you don't mind me correcting you, Manny, but, yes… sometimes it can hurt to try!"

"Sorry about that, Stretch," said Manny. "Wait a minute – where's Felipe?"

With a big groan, Felipe pried himself out from under the bulletin board.

"Here's a bulletin: I think we need to add 'Clean up Turner's Bad Idea' to Stretch's work schedule!"

Rusty surveyed the mess and started to worry. "Now what are we going to do?!"

"Well, the first thing we need to do is to buy a stronger hook – especially if you guys plan on coming up with more great ideas."

Manny chuckled. "Good thing that we were heading to Kelly's this morning anyway."

"We were?" asked Turner.

"Ah, yes, let me inform those who weren't lucky enough to have the work schedule – oh, and an entire bulletin board – land on their faces," Felipe wisecracked. "We're scheduled to help Kelly set up for her super sale this morning!"

On their way to Kelly's Hardware Store, Manny and the tools saw Mr Lopart jogging along the pavement.

"Buenos días, Mr Lopart," greeted Manny.

Mr Lopart was out of breath. "Hoo! Good…day…to… you… too… Manny," he said, stretching from side to side.

"What are you doing, Mr Lopart?" asked Squeeze.

"Warming up!" explained Mr Lopart. "I want to make sure I'm the first one through the door at Kelly's super sale today. That way I can get the best bargains!"

"Hey that's where we're going – to Kelly's Hardware Store," said Dusty.

Mr Lopart was alarmed. "WHAT? You're going there now? B-b-b-but the sale doesn't start until ten o'clock!"

"Don't worry," Manny assured him. "We're just getting there early to help Kelly set up for the super venta – the sale!"

"Super!" exclaimed Mr Lopart. "See you at the venta!"

115

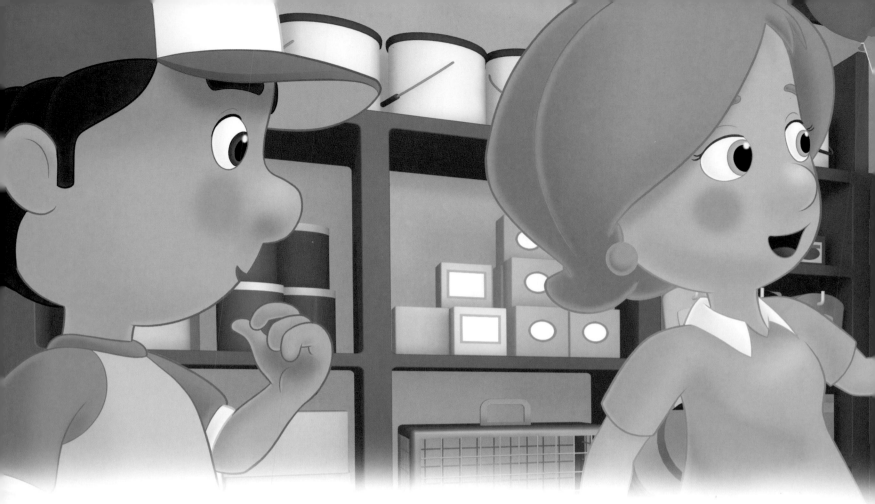

"I'll be with you in a second, guys," Kelly said when Manny and the tools entered her hardware store. "All right, let's go over it one more time, Elliot. If someone asks for a part, and you don't know where it is, what do you do?"

"Um, just a second…it's coming to me…" Elliot thought hard as he tapped two pencils against the counter like drumsticks.

"You look it up in the parts catalogue, right?" Kelly reminded him.

"Yeah, totally!" said Elliot. "That's all I need to know, right?"

"No, Elliot, then you've got to find the part and ring it up on the cash register, remember?" said Kelly.

Elliot started to blush. "Oh, yeah, I always forget that part."

Kelly turned to Manny and the tools. "Elliot's going to help me with the sale today."

"That's great!" Squeeze beamed. "We're helping out too, right?"

"Yes! I need you guys to fasten my brand-new display to the wall," Kelly explained. "It would be a big disaster if it fell."

"Don't worry, Kelly. We have a lot of expertise when it comes to disasters and things falling," Felipe joked. "Right, Turner?"

"Argh, that joke was a disaster," Turner said with a snort.

"Speaking of disasters, we need to buy a strong hook for our bulletin board," Rusty said.

"No problem!" said Kelly. "I was just going to grab a quick breakfast before the sale starts, but I'm sure Elliot could help you with that."

"Me? Oh, I d-d-don't know," Elliot sputtered. "I mean, if this were a skateboard store or a drum shop, I might be able to help them out. But hardware supplies?"

"You'll do fine, Elliot," Kelly promised as she headed for the front door. "Besides, with Manny as your first customer, how hard could it be? I'll be back before you know it. Bye, guys!"

Elliot stood for a while and just looked at Manny nervously. "Um, m-m-may I help you?" he said finally.

"Yes. The bulletin board at my workshop fell down today, so we need a stronger hook to hold it up," Manny explained. Elliot froze, unsure what to do. "Uh, maybe you should look it up in the parts catalogue?" Manny suggested.

"Right, of course!" Elliot grabbed a catalogue from the counter and searched through it. "Hook, hook...Oh, here it is: 'Hook, Charles...1130 Leeside Lane'!"

"I think that might be the phone book, Elliot," Manny offered.

"Heh, I guess you could say that the hardware business just isn't his calling!" Turner whispered to Felipe.

Elliot finally found the parts catalogue, but it wasn't long before he dropped the heavy book on his foot!

"Here, let me help you with that," Manny said, picking up the catalogue and finding the page Elliot needed. After reading the part's description, Elliot ran to the stockroom to find the right hook.

"Found it!" Elliot declared, proudly handing the hook to Manny.

"Yep, that's it. Great job, Elliot," said Manny.

"Cool, dude – oops, I mean, Manny. Well, thanks for stopping by. See you soon!" Elliot said, waving goodbye to Manny.

"Um, aren't you going to ring up our purchase on the cash register?" asked Felipe.

Elliot was disappointed. "Bummer! I knew I forgot something. I'm so totally bad at this!"

"Está bien! It's all right, Elliot," assured Manny. "Everybody makes mistakes when they're learning something new."

"But this many?" Elliot moaned.

"The kid's got a point." Turner grunted.

"Well, the important thing is to learn from your mistakes…so you can be ready the next time," said Manny.

Elliot began ringing up Manny's purchase at the cash register. "That'll be five hundred pounds, please!"

Manny couldn't believe his ears. "For a hook? Are you sure?"

"Oops, my fault! I read it wrong. It's actually just five pounds."
As Elliot fumbled with the keys for the cash register, his sleeve got caught in the register's drawer. "Aw, man, now I'm stuck!"

Squeeze jumped into action and helped yank Elliot's sleeve out of the register drawer. Elliot looked frazzled.

Manny was concerned. "Elliot, are you all right?"

"Aw, it's no use. I can't do this! If it's not a skateboard or a drum set, I'm completely useless," Elliot said with a sigh.

"Don't be so hard on yourself, Elliot," Dusty said.

"You just need a little confidence," added Turner.

"Turner's right," agreed Manny. "You just have to believe in yourself."

"Well, how can I do that?" wondered Elliot.

"It's easy," reasoned Felipe. "If you look confident, you'll feel confident. And if you feel seguro, you'll be seguro."

But at that moment, Elliot just couldn't look or feel very confident at all. "I can't believe one dude can mess up so much," he said, shaking his head.

Stretch had an idea. "You know, I always heard that if you do something that you're good at, confidence is sure to follow. So why don't you go get your skateboard?"

Manny looked nervous. "Um, I don't think skateboarding in Kelly's shop is such a good idea, Stretch."

"Don't worry, I know what I'm doing." Stretch beamed.

But their conversation was interrupted by a huge CRASH! Elliot had collided with the new shop display.

Elliot couldn't believe his eyes. He started to panic. "Oh, no! I made things even worse, and Kelly's going to be back any minute. What am I going to do?"

"Hang on a second, Elliot. I have an idea," said Manny. "You know, the balance you showed on your skateboard might just come in handy for piecing that display back together!"

"Really?" Elliot was shocked.

"Yes, and that drumming of yours is perfect for using a hammer, such as Pat," Manny explained.

"Are you saying that I could actually fix the shelf before Kelly gets back? ME?" Elliot asked in disbelief.

"Well, with a little help, I don't see why not," said Manny. "You just have to believe in yourself."

The fact that Manny believed Elliot was capable of fixing the display gave Elliot the confidence to try. Using a shelf like a skateboard, Elliot rounded up all of the spray paints that fell on the floor by "skating" them back to the display area.

Then, with Pat's help, Elliot put his drumming skills to work and hammered the shelves back into place.

Manny and the tools worked quickly to put all the
hardware supplies back into Kelly's display…just as she had them originally.
When he stepped back to look at the final result, Manny
congratulated Elliot on the great work he had done. "Muy bien, Elliot. Very
good! See? You have more talents than you thought you did!"

"You're right. I should have believed in myself all along,"
said Elliot. "Thanks, Manny. Thanks, tools."

Just then, Kelly returned to the shop. "I'm back! Any problems while I was gone?"

"Nothing I couldn't handle," Elliot replied with a big grin.
"Uh, with a little help from my friends, that is!"

Kelly was pleased. "Thank you, Elliot. You did a great job.
Oh, it's almost ten o'clock! I'd better open the store for business."

As soon as Kelly opened the front door, Mr Lopart came charging in at top speed. "You see? I told you I'd be the first one through the door for the super saaaaaaale!" Mr Lopart tripped over Manny's toolbox and landed on the floor!

"Well, that was a super sail – you sailed right into my toolbox!" joked Manny.

Elliot laughed. "Guess it's not just the prices that are falling today, huh?"

Music of the Meadow

This is Rocket. He takes us anywhere we want to go. And you never know what special tool he'll use next to help us with our missions!

The meadow seems like a very quiet and calm place. But did you know that the meadow is filled with music?
And you can help us find it.
Let's go on an adventure. Let's explore the meadow together.
So come with us!

Welcome to the meadow. Look! It's a bee! It has come to visit. Listen...do you hear something? The bee is making a buzzing sound. Can you buzz like the bee?

Buzz

Buzz

Buzz

Honeybees do a special dance. That is how they tell the other bees where the yummy nectar is. What is your honeybee dance?

Look! It's a flower! It is very pretty. Listen…do you hear something? The flower sways and rustles softly in the wind. Can you sway like the flower?

Swaaayyy

See these tiny little seeds? The rain and sunshine helps them grow into beautiful flowers.
This red flower is my favourite. Which one is your favourite?

Look! It's a stream! It is cool and clear. Listen…
do you hear something? The water is swishing and splashing over
the rocks. Can you swish and splash like the stream?

Rub your hands together.

Swish
Swish
Swish

The water feels cool on
my toes. Do you like to feel
water on your toes?

Look! It's a frog! It is sitting near the water.
Listen…do you hear something? The frog croaks to say hello.
Can you croak like a frog?

Frogs start out as tiny
tadpoles swimming in the water.
Even when they are all grown up,
they still like to swim.

Splash

Look! It's a chipmunk! It is eating a nut.
Listen…do you hear something? The chipmunk is chewing.
Can you chew and chomp like a chipmunk?

I like to eat nuts, too.
Crunch, crunch, crunch.

Chipmunks got their
name because they make a loud
"chipping" sound. Can you "chip"
like a chipmunk?

144

I see a brown chipmunk. Look with me. Can you see that it has black-and-white stripes down its back? How many stripes do you see?

Chip Chip

Chip

45

Look! It's a butterfly! It has landed on a bush.

Listen…do you hear something? The butterfly is drinking.

It sips sweet nectar from the flowers.

Slurp, slurp, slurp. Can you slurp like the butterfly?

The butterfly has its own little built-in straw.

Slurp Slurp Slurp

Someday this caterpillar will change into a beautiful butterfly.

Look! It's a bird and its babies! They are up in a tree. Listen…do you hear something? The bird is singing a sweet song. Can you sing like a bird?

Tap
Tap
Tap

I hear a tap, tap, tap. That's a woodpecker tapping at a tree. It is looking for bugs to eat. Can you tap, tap, tap along with it?

Oh, no! A baby bird has fallen out of the tree.

Don't worry! Rocket is putting the baby bird back in the tree.

Look! It's a grasshopper! It is jumping in the grass. Listen…do you hear something? The grasshopper is chirping. Chirp, chirp, chirp. Can you chirp like a grasshopper?

Grasshoppers make their chirping sound by rubbing a leg over one of their wings.

chirp chirp chirp

Like many insects, grasshoppers have six legs. Their short front legs help them walk. Their long back legs help them jump! Ooops! There it goes!

Chirp

Chirp

Chirp

Look! It's sunset! Our day is ending. Listen…do you hear something? Shhhhh. Many parts of the meadow are sleeping. But others are just waking up! There are crickets chirping. Moths fluttering. Bats flapping. And owls saying who, who, who.

There's always a symphony here in the meadow!

Buzz
Splash
Chip
It's time to say goodbye.
We loved spending time with you. We saw and heard so many things!

We've got a mission!

Also available in the series...

Storybook Collection

Storybook Collection

Storybook Collection

Storybook Collection